Christmas Chaos in Little Valley

The Amish Lantern Mystery Series
Book 6

By Mary B. Barbee

Editing Team: Molly Misko and Jenny Raith

Cover Design by Daniela Colleo of Stunning Book Covers

https://marybbarbee.com

Dedicated to those who believe in the magic of sleigh bells, snowflakes, and the irresistible charm of a small town mystery, may this cozy Christmas Chaos in Little Valley transport you to a world where holiday cheer and sleuthing collide.

"The waves of death engulfed me; the currents of chaos overwhelmed me."

2 Samuel 22:5

Chapter One

Beth rested her elbows on the table and lifted her cup of tea to her face. Leaning in, she inhaled her favorite aroma of peppermint. She closed her eyes and remained silent for a moment, willing the scent to energize her mood.

"*Gut* tea, huh, *Schwester*?" Anna said as she took a sip. Anna looked like Beth's mirror image, sitting across from her, but looks can be deceiving. Anna would insist that she was the more level-headed sister, but Beth would argue that because she liked to take her time and think things through, she was actually the more practical sister.

Anna would most likely then correct Beth's choice of wording and insist that her sister was entirely too analytical. Inevitably the argument would end with an agreement when one of them would give in and shower the other with compliments. They weren't only sisters; they were best of friends.

The sisters were mostly inseparable in their daily lives. They lived next door to each other, their matching small houses built on the same plot of land. Anna and Beth were each married and each had children, but they found ways to see each other and spend time together every single day. Their lives were intertwined, and together, they had established a reputation as the wise women in their Amish community.

Members of the community would often visit or stop them on their walks to ask their help with solving some problem, whether it was how to keep their cookies from spreading on the pan, recommendations for how to get their hens to lay more eggs, or even seeking advice on personal relationships.

Over the past year, their reputation as amateur sleuths had grown in their small town. As the town of Little Valley had been hit with crime after crime, Anna and Beth were inevitably involved with bringing the criminals to justice in one way or another. The town's sheriff, Mark Streen, had grown to trust and respect the sisters, and appreciated their wisdom as much as anyone else.

But today, things were calm and peaceful. A blanket of snow covered the ground, and the house was warm and cozy with a small fire burning slowly in the fireplace just a few feet away from where Anna and Beth sat drinking their tea.

"You know I love peppermint tea all year long," Beth responded to Anna, "but there is just something extra special about it in the winter. Don't you think?"

Anna nodded. "I do love this time of year."

Beth agreed and set her cup down after taking another sip.

"How are you holding up?" Anna asked Beth.

Beth knew what her sister was referring to her oldest daughter, Abigail, moving to another town north of Little Valley.

"I'm doing okay," Beth said with a sigh. "No matter how I try to look at it in a positive light, I can't honestly get around how much I am going to miss seeing Abigail every week or more."

Anna's eyes were kind, and she reached out and touched Beth's arm gently.

"I'll be alright though," Beth said. "I've got to be." She straightened her back as if to show Anna that she would be strong and get through this.

"Well, you know I'm here if you need anything," Anna said, standing to clear the table. She carried the teacups to the sink and with her back turned, she asked Beth what her plans were for the day.

"I'm cleaning house today and pulling together a grocery list," Beth began, counting on her fingers as she listed off the tasks.

"Oh, and I'm going to the library. I am completely out of books already," Beth said. "I am excited to see if they have any more of the garden mystery books I've fallen in love with lately."

"Mmmm... gardening. Even though the snow is pretty, I do miss playing in my flower gardens," Anna said. "What are the mysteries about?"

"Oh, they're each different based on which book you're reading, of course," Beth explained excitedly, "but they always involve some sort of caper around flowers or plants. It's such a fun read!"

"And I bet you solve the mystery before the end of the book every single time," Anna said.

Beth grinned. "Well, that's why I like them so much," she chuckled.

"When was the last time you went to the library? Did you see Greg? How is he doing?" Anna asked, as she dried her hands on her apron and turned to lean on the counter.

"*Ach ja*, he is always there when I go," Beth said. "He always thinks I'm you." Beth grinned at her sister.

Anna rolled her eyes. "After all these years.." her sentence trailing off as she smoothed out her apron in front of her.

The twins had known Greg Wilson since they were children, and at one point, he seemed to have a harmless crush on Anna that never led to anything.

Beth stretched her arms over her head. "Well, it looks like it's going to be a nice quiet Christmas this year," she said.

Anna nodded. "You know, I think you're right. We could use a quiet Christmas, though, after what we've been through this year."

"It's true," Beth said. "Calm instead of chaos for a change. That sounds good to me. I'd be happy to just leave the mysteries in the books for a while."

Chapter Two

The heavy wooden door let out a loud screeching noise as Beth pulled the elaborately carved handle towards her. She wrinkled her brow and squinted one eye as if the sound hurt her ears.

"Wow," she said under her breath. "Noah should come take a look at that." She glanced up at the brass hinges as it closed behind her.

"Welcome to the Little Valley Library," a voice called out, monotonous and dry. Beth turned towards the front desk situated a few yards in front of her. She readjusted the straps of her heavy tote bag on her shoulder and lifted her hand in a quick wave.

A woman whom Beth recognized sat stiffly on a high stool behind the counter, a book open in her hands. She glanced up for only a half-second before returning to her book.

Francine Waters had been the library assistant for the past couple years. Beth couldn't put her finger on what it was, but she wasn't sure how she felt about her. "Good morning, Francine," Beth said politely. Approaching the counter, Beth lifted the borrowed books out of her tote bag and set them down on the counter in front of her. "I'm returning these today."

Francine's hair was tied up in a large messy bun, and small cat-eye shaped glasses sat perched on her tiny nose. Francine had mentioned to Beth during a recent visit that she had just celebrated her fifty-second birthday, and Beth had instantly thought the woman looked and acted older than her age.

She put her finger up in the air in front of her as if to tell Beth to wait just a minute. Her eyes were cast down, and she seemed engrossed in her book. Then, after a few moments, she turned the page and placed a bookmark in between the open pages before closing the book. She sighed and set the book down on the counter.

"Hi, Mrs. Troyer," Francine said flatly. "Thank you for returning your books. Are you looking for anything new today?" She uttered the words as if she were trained to repeat the phrase to each customer one hundred times a day.

"Ah, yes, I'll be looking for a book on caring for new tea roses, a book with Christmas stories for children, and of course, another cozy mystery or two. The last one I read was just wonderful. I could hardly put it down, but of course, I knew who the murderer was well before the end." Beth rambled.

Francine's face was a blank stare, and Beth wondered if she had even heard anything she said.

"Okay. Do you need help finding any of that?" Francine asked, sounding hopeful that Beth would decline assistance.

"Oh, no," Beth said. "Thank you, but I know this library like the back of my hand. Plus, part of the fun is in the browsing."

"Umhmm," Francine nodded as she silently checked in each of Beth's returned books. When finished, Beth thanked her again and headed off towards the children's books section.

One of the things Beth loved about the Little Valley library was that each section was designed to look exactly like the genre of books it stored. The children's books section was colorful and bright with fun decorations placed low on the endcaps of the shelves. There were also cardboard clouds and a large shining sun hanging from the ceiling and the walls were painted stripes of blue, yellow, and pink. Beth's children used to love visiting the library with her when they were younger. They would sit on the small couch or the large floppy beanbag chairs and travel to places all over the world through the books they chose as Beth wandered to find her own books.

A display of books for Christmas was out in the middle of the reading area, easy to spot. Beth immediately found a large book of traditional Christmas stories to read to the younger children during the holidays. She slipped it into her bag and headed toward the gardening section, saving the most desired mystery book selection for last.

The gardening books were set apart from the rest, which Beth preferred. The bookstore in town had the gardening books and the craft books and the cookbooks all grouped together in one section, and Beth thought this was pre-posterous. She gently touched the leaves of the potted aloe plant placed on the shelf next to the books about succu-lents and smiled. *How perfectly placed that is*, she thought to herself.

Before looking for a book about caring for her tea ros-es, she walked around admiring all of the other beautiful plants in the gardening books section. A peace lily and a spider plant were perched on top of the bookcases, beautiful and healthy. English ivy hung from a pot hanging with a beautiful macrame potholder. She remembered when her friend Rachel had made the potholder and donated it to the library some years ago, and she was happy to see it was still in wonderful shape. A large leafy cast iron plant and a striped leaf Chinese evergreen plant were sharing a plant stand in the corner. Beth had helped the librarian, Greg Wilson, select the plants almost a decade before, and it made her so happy to see that they were each happy and thriving in their special home.

Turning her attention back to the books, she focused on her mission. She couldn't find a book about caring for tea roses specifically, but she found a rather large book that covered everything about all kinds of roses. Beth was confident that both she and her sister would enjoy reading all about the flowers and find it helpful when planning and preparing for Spring planting.

She slipped the book into her tote bag and headed across the library to the mystery books, passing the front desk along the way. As she approached, she couldn't help but hear Francine's phone conversation.

"Yeah, that's crazy. Am I in danger working here?" Francine's voice was no longer monotone.

Beth slowed her pace instinctively. She knew it wasn't right to eavesdrop, but she was immediately concerned.

"Okay," Francine continued after pausing briefly. "Are you on your way, though? I have a hair appointment at two o'clock, and I don't want to be late."

Beth looked at the clock on the wall over the desk. It was one-thirty. Beth assumed it was Greg Wilson that Francine was chatting with, so she would take her time selecting her last few books so that she could visit with him before she left.

Francine hung up the phone and picked up her book, settling back onto her stool and escaping back into her story. Beth made her way to the mystery book section on the west wall.

The mystery section was tucked away in the back corner of the library. It was dimly lit with no natural light, creating a sort of creepy vibe. There was a reading nook with two leather backed chairs and a small table with an antique lamp placed in between them. Candelabras with melted candles of all different sizes were set on top of the bookcases. A unique collection of antique magnifying glasses were placed on different empty spots on the shelves next to the bookends. Beth thought the decorations were perfect, not too scary, but definitely intriguing and mystery-like.

Beth grabbed six different stories that jumped out at her right away and settled into one of the tall backed chairs to start the process of narrowing it down to the two or three books that she would take home. She made it a practice to read the back cover and the first chapter of each book before making her final selection.

She had just opened the last book and started chapter one when she heard the front door's hinges scream out. She jumped and then giggled at herself for getting all caught up in the stories and the surrounding atmosphere.

"Honey, I'm home," Beth heard Greg call out, with a teasing tone.

She heard Francine mutter something in response, but she couldn't make out what she had said. Beth returned her attention to the last book and made her final selection, choosing an Agatha Christie short story about a jewel thief and a novel written by a new author where the story puts a detective in a tricky position to catch someone who is robbing the local church's poor box. She grabbed a piece of paper out of her purse and wrote down the title of a book that would have also come home with her if the busy season of Christmas wasn't right around the corner.

Slipping the two selected books into her tote bag with the others and carefully placing the remaining four books back on the shelves where she found them, Beth headed toward the front desk to check out. As she had hoped, Francine's spot was replaced by Mr. Greg Wilson, but Greg was turned away, filing the books that Beth had returned on the shelves behind him to be returned back to their place after closing.

"Hello, Greg," Beth greeted him, emptying her tote bag onto the counter.

Greg jumped and spun around, his hand on his heart. "Oh, my goodness, you scared me," he exclaimed. "I didn't know anyone was here."

Beth giggled. "Yeah, that reading area in the mystery section is pretty perfectly hidden."

Greg smiled, "It's true. I think that might be my favorite little corner in this place." He reached for the books Beth had stacked in front of her, in order of size, smallest to largest. "Is this everything today?" Greg asked, his eyebrow raised.

"Yes, I'm afraid I won't have much time to read the next few weeks with the holiday," Beth replied.

"Ah, the holidays," Greg agreed, typing on the computer keyboard and then scanning each book. "I haven't really been feeling the holiday spirit this year, to be honest."

Beth furrowed her brow, "Oh, yeah? Why is that? Is there something going on?" She hoped Greg didn't think she was being nosy, but she was honestly curious and concerned.

"I just announced it to the public in the newspaper this morning. We're closing the doors at the end of the year," Greg said, looking up to meet Beth's eyes.

Beth gasped and covered her mouth with her hand. "What! Why" She was shocked and had not expected this at all.

"Well, we're too far behind on our bills, honestly. We used to get funding from the city, but the funding was significantly decreased last summer when the town voted that the money should be allocated toward installing security cameras around Little Valley for safety instead," Greg explained as he ran his hands through his thinning hair.

"I mean, I understand that we've had an increase in crime, and security cameras are pretty important. I want the town to feel safe, of course. But I don't know anything about fundraisers, and the bottom line is that we just can't generate enough money to keep the lights on." Greg shifted his eyes down at his hands clasped in front of him. Beth thought he looked defeated.

"What's more," Greg continued, "is that we keep getting threats in the mail." He looked up, his eyes fighting tears. "I can't believe it. This library has been here for three entire generations, and it has never done anything bad to anyone. It has only been a wonderful contribution to the town of Little Valley. But I'm receiving terrible letters from an anonymous person telling me that I had better shut down or else."

Beth realized that her mouth was hanging open and quickly shut it.

Greg shrugged, "If only the person writing those letters knew that we have to shut down for financial reasons anyway, maybe they'd realize they're wasting their time."

"*Ach du lieva*, have you told Sheriff Streen about the letters?"

"Well, yes, of course," Greg confirmed, "but he is at a dead end with it all and thinks whoever is writing the letters are most likely harmless."

"Harmless? That's absurd," Beth said with conviction. She took a deep breath and smoothed the front of her dress. She opened her mouth to speak when a gray cat suddenly jumped up on the desk between her and Greg. Startled, she stifled what would have been a scream.

Greg quickly grabbed the cat in his arms and apologized. "Oh, my gosh, I'm sorry. I didn't mean to put you on edge with all this." Stroking the cat's back, he continued, "This is my cat. His name is Book. He's very sweet, but clearly has bad timing."

Beth joined Greg in laughter and reached over to pet the cat's head. "Well, nice to meet you, Book," Beth said politely with a grin. "I love your name," she said affectionately.

Then, returning to the topics they were just discussing, she said, "Greg, Anna and I have known you almost our whole lives. I can remember when we first met as young children."

Greg nodded, "Yeah, that feels like a hundred years ago."

Beth chuckled. "Well, we can help you. I know we can. We know a thing or two about planning parties, and although we've never hosted a fundraiser, we can figure it out. Christmas is the perfect time to do that, I would presume."

She began shoving her books back into her tote bag. Hoisting it onto her shoulder, she said, "And we are also pretty good at getting to the bottom of mischief, if I do say so myself. We will check in with the sheriff and see where he left off with things."

Greg blushed. "Oh, Beth, I would feel bad getting the two of you involved in all of my worries."

"Nonsense," Beth responded quickly, waving her hand in the air. "We have a proverb for this exact situation. It says, 'When you dig another out of their troubles, you find a place to bury your own.'" She smiled a warm smile before turning to leave.

Halfway towards the door, she stopped and turned around. "I honestly can't imagine what my life would be like without the Little Valley Library," she said, her hand placed on her heart.

With a nod, she said, "I'll be back in touch very soon. Take care of yourself, Greg Wilson."

The door creaked loudly again as it closed behind her, but Beth didn't even hear it this time. Her thoughts were somewhere else.

Chapter Three

Beth's horse and buggy pulled up to Heaven's Diner just as Eli was dropping off Anna.

"Hi, *Schwester*! Hi, Eli!" Beth called out to her sister and brother-in-law. "Eli, are you able to join us for tea or coffee?"

"Nah, I'm on my way to Levi's. I told him I'd be there at two-thirty, and he's going to be waiting for me. We all have such busy schedules these days, it seems," Eli said, shaking his head.

"*Jah*," Anna agreed, stepping down out of the buggy with Eli's help. "You say that now, but when Spring arrives, you'll look back and wish it was the winter months again."

Eli chuckled, "It's true. 'Many times we are climbing mountains when we ought to be quietly resting.'"

Beth grinned. "I'm not sure I've ever heard that proverb applied quite literally in that way," she teased Eli, "but I can see where you're going with that."

Anna winked at Beth and changed the subject. "*Schwester*, did you bring the cranberry bread for Jessica?"

"*Jah*, thank you for reminding me. The bread is in my buggy. I'm so distracted. I have something really important to tell you!" She turned to retrieve the foil wrapped bread before the sisters said goodbye to Eli and headed to the front door of the diner.

The bell chimed as they entered. Looking around, Beth immediately remembered that someone had recently been murdered here, probably just feet away from where she was standing. She shook her head to clear her thoughts. It was a terrible crime, and the case was solved. She needed to close the case in her mind, as well, and move on.

Anna interrupted her thoughts when she hooked her arm under Beth's elbow and steered her toward the empty booth by the window that always seemed to just be waiting for them.

"Good afternoon, Anna and Beth!" Jessica McLean called out. "I'll be there in just a sec," she said, peeking her head out from the kitchen area.

"No rush!" Anna called back. "We're in no hurry!"

Beth looked around. The dining room was empty except for a young family in a booth by the far wall. A little girl sat in a highchair with her blonde hair pulled up into pigtails. The floor around her was covered in bits of food. She was chattering nonsensical words loudly and giggling as if she were the life of the party. Beth couldn't help but smile as she watched her take one bite of a french fry and throw the rest over her shoulder again and again.

A young boy with a baseball cap looking no older than three years old sat quietly between the toddler and his father, shoveling bites of pecan pie into his mouth as fast as he could chew and swallow.

The mother had to have been no more than twenty five years old, and she looked tired. Her blonde curly hair was long and tangled, and her blue-gray sweatshirt had faded stains around the shoulders. She was trying to quiet the toddler while also listening to her husband, nodding at him while passing french fries to the little girl.

The husband was dressed in a clean suit without a tie. His hair was combed neatly, his eyes looked rested. He was talking over the daughter about what his wife needed to tell the mechanic when she took the car to the garage. Beth noticed she didn't sense any frustration in his voice and considered that this way of communication might just be the norm for those two.

"So?" Anna asked, touching Beth's arm to get her attention. "What is so important?"

"Oh, right," Beth said, her thoughts snapping back to the library. "I just went to the library and, Anna, you're not going to believe this."

Anna took a deep breath. "Hmmm. Everything okay with Greg?"

"They're closing the library at the end of the month!" Beth said, grabbing Anna's arm and leaning in closer.

"Oh, that's a shame," Anna said sincerely. "I know you've got to be upset about that. You love that place!"

"*Jah*, I am upset about it. And I told Greg that we would help him. That we would save the library." Beth's words just fell out of her mouth, and she immediately wished she had phrased that a little bit better.

"Wait. What? What are you talking about?" Anna's eyes widened. "Beth, how exactly are we going to save the library? And before the end of this month? With Christmas just a few weeks away?" She pulled her arm away from Beth's grip.

"Okay, I know. I know it sounds crazy." Beth said, pleading with her eyes for Anna to listen to her ideas. "The library is closing because they ran out of funding and are too far behind with the bills, so I thought we could plan a party and raise some funds to keep it open."

Anna sat silent, slowly shaking her head. Her eyes shifted to look out the window next to them.

"We can totally throw a Christmas party, Anna. I mean, how many Christmas parties have we actually planned in our lives?" Beth asked, still pleading.

"Zero. We've thrown zero Christmas parties outside of our community that are fundraising parties, Beth. I'm sorry, but I think you've gotten in way over your head on this one," Anna said softly.

"Okay, so I know we don't have any experience planning fundraisers, but I'm up for the challenge and I believe we could do it." Beth looked at her sister, hopeful.

Anna sat in silence, biting her lip. "I don't know, Beth. I think that's kind of a big deal."

"What's a big deal?" Jessica's southern accent interrupted the sisters. "Everything okay over here? The two of you look like you're pretty deep in some serious conversation."

Beth smiled at Jessica, relieved to see her. She had not expected Anna's reaction to this idea of hers, and she welcomed the interruption.

"*Gute daag*, Jessica!" Beth said, "It's so good to see you."

Anna nodded, "*Jah*, how are you doing?"

Jessica grabbed a chair from the nearby table and pulled it up to the end of the booth and sat down leaning forward. "Life is really good," she said with a glowing smile.

"Business is good. I'm enjoying spending time with Matthew outside of work, and he still comes in for lunch everyday, too. The best part, though, is that there's no more drama in my life. I like things nice and quiet, I'll tell ya." She winked at Beth.

"Oh, I agree with that," Anna said, shooting a knowing glance at Beth. "I also like things nice and quiet. There is something to say for doing more of less, especially this time of year."

Beth stayed quiet. She knew what Anna was implying.

"Right, the holidays always remind me how important it is to be grateful for the wonderful things in my life. My friends and family, and that includes you two," she said, reaching over and grabbing both of their hands hand and giving a gentle squeeze, "and my diner, my health, my perfect little home... well, the list just goes on and on."

"*Jah*, it is important to be grateful," Beth agreed. "Some people are just full of worry this time of year," she said, matching that knowing look that Anna had sent her minutes before, "and this is the season of giving."

Anna sighed.

"Okay, why do I get the feeling that I'm missing something here?" Jessica asked, sitting straighter in her chair.

"Well, Beth was just telling me that she volunteered the two of us to help the library plan a party to raise funds for them," Anna explained.

Jessica clasped her hands together, "Oh! I love this idea! And I love the Little Valley Library! This is the perfect time of year to throw a fundraising party. You know, my mother-in-law used to throw fundraisers and I helped out with catering and a few other things from time to time. I may be able to help you ladies, if you need it. And Matthew can help with the floral decorations, for sure. Let's see, who else..." Jessica tapped her finger on her chin.

"See, Anna?" Beth exclaimed, squirming in her chair. "It's not a bad idea, and we will probably have lots of help once word gets out that they have to close their doors."

"What?" Jessica asked, shocked. "The library can't close! It's been open so long! What will Little Valley do without a library? That's terrible!"

"I know," Beth said, looking over at Anna. "It simply can't happen."

"Okay, okay," Anna said, a smile hesitantly spreading across her face. "I'm in. Let's get started."

Beth squealed and jumped onto her feet, running over to hug Anna. "Thank you, *Schwester*, I knew you would help!"

Returning to her seat, Beth had a permanent grin on her face. Her stomach was full of butterflies and her mind was racing, already creating plans.

Suddenly the little girl across the room cried out loud and the three women all looked over to find that the mother was on her feet, pulling her daughter out of the chair and into her arms.

"I'll be right back, ladies, with some coffee. Don't go anywhere," Jessica said as she jumped up to take care of her customers.

Beth took a breath and lowered her voice, "Anna, there's something else."

Anna looked at Beth cautiously, "Oh, no. What else could there be, *Schwester*?"

"Well, Greg told me that he has been receiving anonymous threats in the mail to shut the library down. I don't know much more than that, but he assures me he told Sheriff Streen and that the sheriff has hit a dead end with the investigation." Beth felt around for loose strands of hair that might've fallen out of her *kapp*.

"Oh, no," Anna said. And then she repeated them again, her eyes locked with Beth's. "Oh, no."

"*Jah*," Beth continued. "I told Greg that we would go check in with the sheriff and see if we can help."

"Oh, Beth," Anna said, shaking her head before resting her face in the cup of her left hand, elbow propped on the table. "So much for a nice relaxing holiday season, I guess," she said, watching the snowflakes fall one by one.

Chapter Four

S heriff Mark Streen was enjoying the peace and quiet. It was unusual for him to be alone in the office, but his deputy, Christopher Jones, had left early with the sheriff's permission to go help take care of his family who had come down with colds.

Sheriff Streen whistled softly as he settled in his chair with a cup of hot coffee. He opened his inbox and started reviewing all the unread emails that had piled up over the last couple busy months. He had sent twenty-three emails to the inbox folder labeled *Junk* before he was distracted by the clip-clop sound of horses' feet on the pavement. He looked up from his computer to see a familiar horse and buggy slowly entering the parking lot. He smiled as he watched out the large windows from his desk, immediately recognizing the two identical faces sitting side by side in the buggy.

"Well, there goes the peace and quiet," he said, chuckling to himself. He was always glad to see Anna and Beth, but he also knew the twin sisters didn't just pay him an unsolicited visit. He was sure they were there to talk about something on their minds.

He watched as the two women stepped out of their buggy before turning around to collect their things. The sheriff noticed Anna was carrying a pastry box tied shut with a red and green ribbon.

Maybe they're just bringing holiday treats, he thought to himself, as he held the door open and called out warm greetings.

"Well, hello! What a pleasure to see you both!" His smile was broad and sincere. "Happy Holidays," he continued as the sisters filed in, returning the smile.

"Merry Christmas, Sheriff," the twins said almost in unison. The three of them shared small talk for a few minutes, catching up on each others' lives like old friends.

"We brought a mix of sweets for the holiday, for you and Deputy Jones to share," Anna said, handing the sheriff the pastry box.

"Thank you so much," Sheriff Streen said, taking the box and setting it gently on the counter by the coffeemaker. "We love your treats."

"Where is Deputy Jones?" Beth asked.

"He's at home taking care of his family right now. The boys brought home a cold from school a couple days ago, and then his wife started feeling badly today. Things are pretty quiet around here, so I sent him home early."

"Ah, we'll keep them in our prayers," Beth said.

Beth and Anna looked at each other, and Sheriff Streen knew then that his first instincts were right. The sisters weren't just there to deliver treats.

"What's on your mind, ladies?"

Beth leaned forward, her eyes bright. The sheriff couldn't deny that Beth and Anna were integral parts of solving recent criminal cases over the past year and a half, and he recognized the twinkle in Beth's eye. He knew how much she loved being a part of an investigation.

"I talked to Greg Wilson at the library yesterday," Beth said.

The sheriff knew immediately where she was going with this.

"Ah, here we go," he said, raising his hand as if to tell Beth to say no more. "You're here about the letters the library has been getting."

Beth nodded.

"We don't have much of anything to go on," the sheriff said. "As a matter of fact, I was headed out there tomorrow to return the letters to Greg. We sent the first couple letters into the lab for a DNA check on the envelope, but there were no circumstantial results."

"So, you don't have any leads at all?" Beth asked, her forehead creased.

"Not at this time, no," the sheriff confirmed. "I'm not too worried about them right now, either, to be honest. I'm not sure what Greg told you, but the letters have been coming for a couple months now and nothing else has happened."

"*Jah*, Greg told me that you thought they were harmless," Beth said.

The sheriff shrugged. "I can't say for sure, of course, but since nothing else has happened, and we don't have any positive identification, then there isn't a whole lot we can do."

Anna nodded.

Beth fidgeted in her seat, squeezing her hands together in her lap and crossing her legs at the ankles.

"Did you question anyone about the letters, Sheriff?" Beth asked.

"Why do I feel like I should ask if you have any leads?," the sheriff grinned.

Beth shrugged. "I haven't even seen the letters," she said.

"Right," the sheriff responded, standing to retrieve the letters from the locked metal safe on the back wall. "Silly me," he teased. "I probably should've come to the two of you sooner, honestly." He pulled a file folder out of the safe and left the door of the safe open just a crack. "Maybe you'll see something I didn't." He set the folder on the desk in front of them.

Inside the folder were two letters, each individually sealed with their envelopes in a plastic evidence bag, marked with a number and a stamp that read Mainstay County Sheriff's Office. Beth and Anna leaned in to read the first letter together. The words were written by hand neatly, with a mix of cursive and print on a simple piece of lined paper that appeared to have been torn from a notepad. Beth read the letter aloud.

To Whom It May Concern,

It is time for the library to shut its doors.

For good.

You have until the end of the month to announce to the town that you are closing, or you will regret it.

"There is no signature," she said. She turned the bag over to take a closer look at the envelope. It was addressed with the same cursive-print handwriting as was used on the letter.

"Well, that's pretty simple and to the point," Anna said aloud.

"*Jah*," Beth agreed, turning the letter over to reveal the next in the stack. It contained the same handwriting and used the same type of paper as the first. She read the next letter aloud, as well.

To Whom It May Concern,

I still have not heard any announcement of your closure. Surely, you don't think I am bluffing?

Consider this a threat: If you don't announce to the town in the next week that you are shutting your doors then we will force your hand and shut it down ourselves.

"Still no signature," Beth said.

The sheriff watched the twins as they read the letters. It's true he had seen this sort of thing, threats sent by letter, in his younger years when he worked in the nearby metropolitan city, and more often than not, the letters turned out to be young kids daring each other to do something stupid, or another sort of hoax of some kind. It didn't make sense to him that someone would gain anything from the local library shutting down.

"Well, it's interesting that they use the word 'we' here," Beth said.

Anna nodded. "And they definitely sound a bit more angry in this second letter," she said, looking at her sister.

Beth raised her eyebrows as glanced at the sheriff sitting across from her.

"Other than receiving the letters, has anything else weird happened at the library?" Beth asked.

The sheriff shook his head. "Nothing that has been reported," he said. "And these letters arrived more than a few weeks ago. I think it has been like six weeks since the first arrived, and the second came a couple weeks later."

Beth turned the second letter over to find an envelope similar to the first.

"No stamp either," the sheriff mentioned.

"*Jah*, that is odd," Beth said. "So, how did Greg get the letters?" she asked.

"He said they were in the mailbox with the rest of the mail," Sheriff Streen responded.

Beth and Anna stared at the letters a few more moments.

"Anything y'all see that I'm missing?" the sheriff asked, hopeful.

Beth was quiet for a moment and then, tracing with her index finger, she said, "I'm just looking at the long slender loops below the use of the letter "y" and how the letter "s" was always a printed curved line instead of a boxy cursive letter." She looked up from the letter. "I'm no handwriting analyst, of course, but it looks like that's the only thing we have to go on here."

"*Jah*, there's nothing really special about the paper or ink or anything, I would say," Anna said, agreeing with her sister. "It's definitely a mystery."

The sheriff nodded. "Yep, and I read the announcement in the paper yesterday, so it's likely that the letters will stop now without any harm," he said.

"Ah, that's what you meant by the letters being harmless," Anna said, putting the pieces together in her head.

Beth leaned back in her chair, and looked slowly from Anna to the sheriff and back to Anna again. She shook her head.

"I don't know what it is," she said, "but something tells me it's not going to be that easy." She smoothed out her skirt with the palms of her hands and looking down, she added, "Especially when whoever wrote these letters finds out we're throwing a fundraiser party to save the library."

Sheriff Mark Streen sat up taller in his chair.

"Wait. What?" he asked, confused. "You're trying to save the library?"

Anna and Beth nodded slowly in unison, looking like doubles sitting in front of him.

"Well, that's the first I've heard about this," he said, removing his cowboy hat and running his hands through his thinning hair.

Here we go again, he thought to himself.

Chapter Five

Anna held on tight to the handle of the buggy door as the horses walked at a steady pace down Main Street. No matter what, she would be forever nervous riding in a horse and buggy driven by her sister since the wreck that nearly killed them both.

"I hope we remembered everything," Beth said, purposely ignoring Anna's unnecessary white-fisted grip.

"Well, you made the list and we checked it twice," Anna joked.

Beth chuckled and glanced over at her sister with a grin. She thought the joke about Santa must be a good sign that her sister was not only onboard with planning this holiday party she had been roped into, but she just might be enjoying it, too.

The buggy pulled to a stop in front of the library, and Anna and Beth carefully stepped down onto the snowy ground. Beth pulled her cape tighter around her shoulders, attempting to protect herself from the cold wind and snow swirling in the air.

"It is really blustery today," Beth said loudly to Anna who had her purse on her arm and was headed for the front door, her shoulders slumped forward and her gloved hands holding her winter cap tightly in place.

Beth tied up the horse quickly and followed her sister. Anna pulled the door open and looked up at the squeaking hinges.

"I see what you mean," she said, referring to the comment Beth had made earlier about someone needing to take a look at the loud hinges.

Right away, Beth noticed the Christmas tree set up by the front door. It smelled of fresh pine and sat tall but bare, secured in a simple metal Christmas tree stand placed directly on the floor.

"They need something under that," Beth noted to Anna, pointing it out to her.

"*Jah*, we can maybe find some plastic around here to put under it," Anna said.

"And surely they have a tree skirt," Beth said.

"Well, let's go see," Anna said, lifting her hand to wave at Greg who had just noticed their arrival. He had come around the corner from the back, a stack of books in his arms.

"Hello, Anna and Beth!" Greg said, cheerily, leaning forward to slide the books onto the counter. "How do you like our Christmas tree? I thought we can't have a Christmas party without a Christmas tree, right?" He smiled, and Beth was glad to see that his spirits had been lifted since the last time she saw him.

"Right," Beth said. "It was on our list, so we're glad to see you're on the same page!"

"Do you have a tree skirt and ornaments?" Anna asked, as she approached the counter and set her purse down on a table next to it.

"Not yet," Greg said.

"No worries," Anna said, as she waved her hand in the air. "We have extras."

Just then, Beth felt something brush against her ankle. She looked down to find Book walking around with her tail in the air, venturing from sister to sister. Beth knelt to pet her, clicking her tongue softly to get her attention.

"Aw, what a cute kitty," Anna said.

"*Jah*, her name is Book," Beth explained.

"That's fitting," Anna chuckled.

"Yeah, she's been working here for a few years now," Greg joked. "She holds all the secrets of the library."

"Speaking of secrets, Greg," Beth said, straightening up, "Anna and I paid a visit to the sheriff and asked about the letters."

"Ah," Greg said. "Anything new with the investigation?"

Beth shook her head. "It doesn't sound like it, but we were able to take a look at the letters and will give them some thought."

"Thank you," Greg said, a look of gratitude in his eyes. "It should all be a moot point now, though, since I announced the closing of the library, like the person writing the letters wanted."

"Well, we might cause some more trouble with the fundraiser," Anna pointed out.

"Oh, that's true," Greg said. A shadow of worry quickly crossed his face.

"We'll get to the bottom of it though," Beth interjected. "They can't hide behind those letters forever."

"Especially when we invite the whole town to the party," Anna continued.

Greg sighed. "I don't know if I'm ready for this," he said.

"Ready for what?" Francine asked as she entered the room from the back of the library.

"The Christmas fundraising party," Anna responded.

"Oh, right," Francine said. "Y'all are still doing that, huh?"

"Yes," Beth said, her voice short and stern. She didn't appreciate Francine casting a gloomy slump on the party plans, and she wished she had the day off and left them to do the planning without her.

"Well, let's get started meeting," Anna said. Beth assumed she was trying to steer the conversation away from Francine. "Where shall we sit?"

Greg ushered the women to the table off to the side of the front area and offered them water or tea. They both requested water and Greg scurried off to grab their drinks for them. As he passed Francine, he offered for her to join them, but Francine declined politely.

"Not if I don't have to," she said. "If it's okay with you, I'm going to finish up so I can get out of here a little early. Cassidy's father is dropping her off anytime now, and I want to take her to dinner."

"Oh, good. I haven't seen Cassidy in ages," Greg said. "Sure, finish up here and go have fun." He headed to the kitchen.

Anna and Beth settled in at the table. Beth pulled her notebook out of her purse, and clicked her pen, prepared to start writing. She crossed off *Christmas tree*.

The front door opened and a young teenage girl walked in, snowflakes dangling on the ends of her long dark curls.

"Hi, Mom," she called out, sauntering towards the counter. She glanced over at Anna and Beth and quickly looked away.

"Hi, baby," Francine said without raising her eyes toward her daughter. "I'm finishing up. You'll have to sit and wait. Maybe do some homework."

Cassidy sighed and rolled her eyes. "But I'm so hungry," she whined.

"Well, it's not my fault if your father didn't give you a snack," Francine snapped at her.

Cassidy ignored her mother's comment and disappeared behind the shelf of the mystery section of the library.

Greg finally came from the back of the library with glasses of water and a cup of coffee for himself. He caught a glimpse of Cassidy tucked away in the little nook, surrounded by books. He stopped and smiled.

"Hi, Cassidy! How are you?" Greg asked, excited to see her.

Beth could hear Cassidy respond, "Good, Mr. Wilson. How are you?"

"I'm good, thank you! You've grown just since I saw you last, I think," Greg continued. "Did you see I hung your art over there by the art and music section?"

Cassidy came around from behind the shelves to peer across the room in the direction where Greg nodded. Beth looked up and followed their gaze to see a beautiful drawing of a vase with a bouquet of sunflowers.

"Oh, my gosh, that's nice, Mr. Wilson, but that's so old. My art is much better than that now," she said with a small smile.

"Well, you'll have to give me something newer, I guess," Mr. Wilson responded.

"I thought the library was shutting down," Cassidy said, glancing over at her mother who was oblivious to the conversation, eyes switching back and forth from the computer screen to a pile of books on the counter in front of her.

Mr. Wilson hesitated. His smile faded.

"Well, I don't know if you've met Mrs. Miller and Mrs. Troyer," he nodded towards Anna and Beth and began walking towards them. "But, they are planning a fundraising party that might raise enough money to save the library."

Beth looked over just in time to see Cassidy shrug her shoulders and mumble, "Sounds good," before turning around and walking off towards her previous spot.

Mr. Wilson turned around and carefully set the cup of coffee and glasses of water down on the table and smiled an apologetic smile at Anna and Beth.

"Well, shall we start to review the list?" Beth asked, wanting to change the subject and start the planning process.

"I'm all ears," Greg said as he took a sip of his coffee.

Just as Beth and Anna and Greg were beginning to discuss the selection of treats, Francine and Cassidy were gathering their things, pulling on hats and scarfs, and heading towards the front door.

"I'm headed out, Greg," Francine said.

Greg looked up from the list in front of him and waved.

"Be safe, you two!" He called out as Francine mumbled something to her daughter.

"Oh! Mr. Wilson," Cassidy said interrupting her mother. "Dad told me to tell you to bring your guitar to the theater tomorrow night."

Francine clutched her daughter's arm and turned her back toward the door. This time, she could be heard clearly when she snapped, "You're not your father's messenger, Cassidy."

Beth, Anna and Greg remained silent as Francine pushed the door open and escorted her daughter outside.

"Sorry about that," Greg apologized. "Cassidy's a good kid, but her parents just don't get along very well."

"Well, we've raised a few teenage girls ourselves," Anna said. "And I'm sure it's not easy to co-parent."

Greg sighed. "I'm sure you're right, especially when the parents *really* don't like each other."

Beth instantly felt sad for Cassidy. She glanced over at Cassidy's drawing and thought to herself, *I wonder what her more recent art looks like.*

Chapter Six

B eth finished loading the buggy with the last of the supplies for the party. She glanced up at the light blue sky and marveled at how the snow capped trees served as a beautiful contrast with such perfection. The days were shorter and the moon was already hanging high above them.

"You got everything?" Anna asked from the front porch.

"I think so!" Beth said, cheerily. It had been a few days since they had met with Greg at the library and everything was coming together perfectly. The invitation to the party had been posted in the paper despite the last minute notice, and the kids in the community pitched in and tacked flyers around town. They were expecting a big turnout, so Anna and Beth had recruited their oldest daughters, Sarah and Abigail, to help with the setup today, along with Jessica McLean when she could steal away from the diner after the dinner rush.

Sarah and Abigail pulled up in Abigail's buggy just as Anna was slipping on her gloves.

"Great timing!" Beth called out with a wave.

Abigail and Sarah stepped down onto the snow covered gravel and headed towards Beth and her buggy. Anna secured her front door behind her and carefully stepped down the front porch steps to greet her daughter and niece.

"Oh, this is so much fun!" Anna said, her voice full of excitement.

Beth grinned, remembering how Anna previously didn't even want to be a part of this.

"*Jah*, we're looking forward to it! I just love being back with all of you for the holidays," Abigail said, a broad smile spreading across her face as she finished hugging her mother and aunt. "Do we need to put anything in my buggy?"

"*Nae*, I think everything fits in here," Anna said, pointing to Beth's packed full buggy.

"Okay! We're all set then," Sarah said. "Let's get out of this snow. We'll follow you to the library."

"Sounds *gut*," Beth said, hoisting herself up into the buggy and settling in. Anna went around to the passenger side and climbed in, getting settled next to her sister. Beth reached over and squeezed Anna's gloved hand.

"*Denki* for doing this, *Schwester*," Beth said. "I'm not sure I said that yet."

"I'm sorry I made such a big deal out of it," Anna said. "You were right. I am having a good time, and it turned out to be easier than I thought."

"Well, maybe we should make it an annual thing, then," Beth said, with a wink.

Anna squeezed Beth's hand back and said, "Don't get carried away." She chuckled, "Why don't we just see how this goes first."

Beth grinned and then grabbed the reins, snapping them to give the signal to her horse to start walking. After getting on the road, she glanced behind her to make sure that Abigail and Sarah were behind her.

After arriving at the library, it was all hands on deck to unload the buggy. Everyone was anxious to get out of the cold and settled in the warm library.

"*Gute mariye!*," Greg called out to the ladies as they carried in the last of the supplies."You should have called me! I would have unloaded all of that for you."

"Nonsense," Beth said. "We have four able bodies here."

"But thank you," Anna said, shooting a quick glance over at her sister.

"I mean, yes, thank you anyway," Beth said, realizing that she might have sounded impolite. Before she could think any more of it, a loud commotion and a short scream erupted from behind the counter. Greg hurried to see what it was as Francine stretched up from below the counter. Her bun was exceptionally messy today and she looked tired. Beth wondered what she could do to help this newly single mother and vowed to come up with something before the holiday season was over.

"Everything okay?" Greg asked.

"Yes," Francine said, sounding irritated. "I was trying to clean up back here when I thought I saw a mouse scurry by." She pointed to the shelves under the counter.

"Oh, goodness," Greg said. "Let me take a look." He came around and stooped down, moving papers and looking thoroughly through the stuff on the shelves. "I don't see anything."

Francine huffed and crossed her arms. "Well, I saw something," she said, sulking. "And if we have mice in here, we are going to have to pass an inspection."

Greg lowered his voice. "I really don't think we have mice in here. I don't see any trace of any." He paused and turned his back to the group, mumbling something to his assistant. She smoothed her hair back from her face and responded in a low voice. "I'm not stressed, Greg. I don't know what Damon is telling you, but I wish you wouldn't talk about me."

"We're not talking about you," Greg said, his voice starting to sound irritated as well, Beth thought to herself.

Wanting to release the tension in the air, Beth corralled Anna, Sarah and Abigail and suggested they decorate the tree. Abigail and Sarah and Anna found the lights and ornaments and began to hang them on the tree. Beth volunteered to set up the extension cord and lay down the tree skirt.

She glanced over at the counter and noticed that Greg and Francine were no longer standing there. *They must've headed to the back*, Beth thought to herself, wondering if Greg was giving in and trying to find some rat poison to put down.

Beth rifled through the boxes to find the extension cord. She gave up on one box and decided she must have put it in one of the canvas bags she had brought. She smiled as she overheard Abigail and Sarah giggling as they remembered decorating Christmas trees together as young girls.

Still looking, Beth thought to herself, *I hope I didn't leave it at home.* She returned to the tree.

"Anna, do you remember packing the extension cord?" she asked. Before Anna could answer, Greg came around the counter from the back of the library.

"Do you need an extension cord?" Greg asked. "I think I might have one in the utility room."

"Oh, okay, *gut*," Beth responded. "I can go get it."

"No," Greg said quickly. "I'll grab it. I'll be right back," and he scurried off, disappearing behind the wall again to head off toward the back.

Beth turned her attention to the tree, and noticing that the women were almost at the bottom of one of the boxes of ornaments, she went to open the next.

As Beth squatted down, she heard Book meow loudly. She turned and said, "*Hallo*, Book. How are you tonight?" Book cozied right up to Beth, brushing against her bent knees and Beth scratched her behind the ears.

Abigail gasped. "Watch out, Mom!" she exclaimed. "That cat has stepped in something, and she's going to get it all over your dress."

Beth quickly stood to her feet, pulling her dress close to her legs. She looked behind the cat and saw red footprints leading all across the front area, leading from the mystery book section. She gasped, too.

"What is it?" Anna asked. "What did she step in?"

"I don't know," Beth said, as she started to walk in the direction of the footprints, Anna, Abigail and Sarah close behind.

As they approached, Greg appeared with an extension cord in hand. When he saw the four of them looking down at the floor, he followed their gaze.

"What *is* that?" he asked, turning to look where the footprints came from, and seeing that they lead out from the mystery book section.

His face went white. He held an arm out to stop the women from advancing any further, and whispered, "Wait here."

The women stopped and watched as Greg tiptoed over to the mystery section. He stifled a scream, and the extension cord dropped to the floor by his feet as he covered his mouth.

"Francine!" he yelled, and he rushed ahead, disappearing behind the shelf. "Call an ambulance!" He called out just a few seconds later.

The room fell silent, and Beth began to run forward. As she approached the end cap on the bookshelf, she grabbed on tight to keep the room from swaying. There, lying on the floor in front of her, was Francine. Book's red footprints led right to Francine's body. Beth watched as Greg tried to administer CPR. She heard Abigail's frantic voice on the phone, talking to the emergency dispatcher.

"Hold on one second," Abigail said. "*Maem*! Is she breathing?" she called out, urgently.

Beth stood in shock as Anna walked up and wrapped her arm around her, turning her away from the bloody scene in front of her.

"Aunt Anna? What should I tell them?" Abigail asked again.

"Tell them to hurry," Sarah said, standing next to her mother, a tear silently rolling down her cheek.

Chapter Seven

Sheriff Streen parked his patrol car and turned off his lights. He checked his cell phone quickly to see if Deputy Jones had returned his call or sent him a text. The screen was blank. As he stepped out of his car, his boots sank into soft snow up to below his ankles. He pulled his beanie tighter around his ears. He mounted the front steps of the library just as the ambulance arrived.

Opening the front door, he saw Anna, Beth, Abigail and Sarah standing near the Christmas tree, huddled in a tight circle. They appeared to be in prayer. Greg Wilson quickly approached the sheriff, out of breath. The sheriff noticed right away that he had blood on his hands and on the cuffs of his sleeves.

"Hold on," Sheriff said. "Stop right there. Keep your hands where I can see them."

Greg stopped immediately and held his hands up shoulder-height. "It's Francine Waters, Sheriff. She's dead. Over there." He motioned with his head and neck. "In the mystery book section."

The sisters and their daughters had all turned to face the sheriff. Beth walked forward.

"Sheriff," Beth said. "Greg tried to save Francine with CPR. That's the blood."

The front door opened and two young paramedics entered with their bags of special tools in hand.

"Body is over here, guys," the sheriff said, leading the way behind the bookshelf. When they approached the body, one of the techs bent on one knee. Beth presumed he was checking for a pulse. After a few moments, she was sure she was right when he stood and shook his head.

"Okay," the sheriff said. "Looks like we're going to need the coroner," he said solemnly. His phone rang, and he answered it.

"Hey, Deputy," he said. "Yeah, I'm at the library now. We have a ten fifty-five." He paused before continuing, "Yeah, it's Francine Waters. Looks like a stab wound, but we'll let the coroner be the judge of that, of course."

Beth and Anna exchanged glances.

Greg stood off to the side, his eyes wet and fixated on his trembling hands in front of him.

Beth leaned over to Anna and whispered, "I think we should ask if Greg can go wash his hands."

Anna nodded, and seeing the sheriff slip his phone back into his pocket, she approached him.

"Sheriff? Okay if Greg goes to clean up?" she asked, politely.

"I'm afraid not," the sheriff said. "I'm actually going to need to take statements from all of you that were here tonight and take some pictures." His voice was cold and stern. Anna nodded and began to walk back to join the others when the sheriff reached out and touched her arm gently.

"Just hang tight, Anna," Sheriff Streen said in a more calming voice. "The deputy is on his way, and we'll get you all out of here and on your way home as soon as we can."

Anna forced a smile and said, "Thank you, Sheriff. We'll wait for your lead."

The sheriff looked over at Greg. "I'll start with Greg," he said, and headed to ask Greg questions, pulling a small notepad out of his chest pocket.

The emergency techs had finished and headed toward the front door. Before leaving, they stopped to tell the sheriff that they had called the coroner. They wished him a good night and pushed the heavy front door open. A bit of snow swirled inside before it closed.

"What should we do, *Maem*?" Abigail asked Beth.

"Let's just go sit down and wait to see what the sheriff might need," Beth said, taking Abigail and Sarah's hands and guiding them over the footprints to the table. She sat Abigail and Sarah with their backs facing the area where Francine's body lay dead. She sat across from them, and Anna joined her, pulling up a chair.

Sarah wiped a tear away. "It's so sad," she said. "She has a daughter."

"I know," Abigail said. "I can't imagine who would do this to a mother, especially this close to Christmas."

Beth leaned in close to Anna and whispered. "Do you realize this happened while we were right here?" Her eyes were wide.

Anna nodded, her face solemn. "I know. I don't understand how we didn't hear anything. She didn't scream or fight back?" Anna whispered back, her face turned away from their daughters.

"It looked to me like she was stabbed in the neck. I don't know if she could've screamed," Beth whispered.

"I guess you're right," Anna said. Her eyes cast down at her hands in her lap.

"We were the only ones here, though," Beth continued whispering. "Except for Greg."

Anna shot a surprised look at Beth. "There's no way," she whispered to Beth.

Before Beth could answer, the front door opened and Jessica entered, stomping her boots on the mat just inside. She looked up and froze, seeing the sheriff talking to Greg and seeing the somber faces of her close friends. The sheriff stepped in front of her, and held his hand up, keeping her from taking another step.

"Jessica, this is a crime scene. I'm afraid you'll have to leave," he explained politely.

"Oh, my goodness, is everything okay? What's going on?" she asked, frantically.

"You'll find out everything soon enough. Just please go on home now," he continued, placing his arm on her back and gently escorting her back outside.

Beth watched as Greg slumped to sit down on the floor, still holding his hands out away from his body as if he didn't want to touch anything. He crossed his legs as a child would sit and rested his forearms on his knees. He swayed back and forth slightly, a blank look on his face.

The door opened and this time, the deputy walked in the room. The sheriff was right behind him. The deputy nodded to the women sitting quietly at the table, and both men glanced over at Greg. The sheriff leaned down to mumble something Beth couldn't hear and Greg nodded.

"Over here," the sheriff said as he led the way to the crime scene. As they passed by the women's table, Beth called out the sheriff's name. The men stopped and looked at Beth.

"Can I please use the restroom?" Beth asked. There was an awkward moment of silence and Beth continued, "I promise I'll be quick."

Sheriff Streen nodded and then continued to lead the way with the deputy on his heels.

Anna looked at Beth, her eyebrows raised.

"I'll be right back," Beth whispered. She stood to her feet. She knew she had to pass the body in order to get to the restroom. She wanted another look at the crime scene now that the shock had begun to wear off. Passing, she glanced over. The men's backs were turned as they discussed what they were seeing.

"Yeah, the coroner's on his way," Beth heard Sheriff Streen explain. "It's such a strange wound, right?"

The deputy nodded. "It is. I'll be interested to see what the coroner says."

As Beth walked briskly by, unnoticed, she spotted a book on the floor near the victim's hand. Something was odd about the shape of the book, but she couldn't tell what it was from her distance, and she was trying hard not to see Francine's pale face. She headed into the bathroom and shut the door, leaning against it for a moment, catching her breath. She headed toward the sink and saw her reflection in the mirror. *I look tired*, she thought to herself. She straightened her *kapp* and smoothed out her apron. As she reached for the faucet to turn on the sink, she froze. She noticed a dark pink liquid in a small puddle at her feet. She stepped back and stooped down, holding up her dress a few inches and saw the liquid dripping onto the floor in front of the closed cabinet.

She straightened up and slowly looked around. Within seconds, she noticed what looked to be bright red blood on the window frame. The window appeared to be unlatched. She grabbed paper towels from the dispenser and used them to open the door, rushing out to the main area.

"Sheriff!" She called out, her tone urgent. "There's something you need to see in here."

Chapter Eight

Greg sat straight up in bed. He was covered in sweat, and his body was trembling and cold. He inspected his hands. There was no blood. It was just another nightmare. He threw his sheets off and reached over to his bedside table, knocking his guitar pick on the floor as he grabbed his water bottle. He chugged the water until it was gone seconds later and then tossed the empty bottle towards his overflowing trash can.

His feet on the floor, his shoulders slumped forward as he headed to the bathroom to take a shower. Ever since that night, he couldn't seem to take enough showers. He remembered coming home and scrubbing his hands, arms, and fingernails until they were sore. He left his stained shirt with the sheriff and wore just a white t-shirt under his coat as he returned home.

Stepping into the shower, Greg let the water wash away his tears as he stood there, his mind filled with hopeless thoughts. His life felt like it was falling apart. His career for the past twenty-eight years was working as the librarian at the Little Valley Library, and now it was all crashing down around him. He didn't know what he would do without it.

As he turned off the shower and reached for a towel, his thoughts shifted to Francine. He hadn't heard back from Damon yet, and he worried about Cassidy. He couldn't wrap his head around her murder. It happened right under his nose, and he had no way to stop it or even help the sheriff find the killer. He wanted to help, but he felt useless.

He dressed and stared at himself in the mirror, his razor in his hand, positioned to start shaving his five o'clock shadow but not moving. He felt frozen, lost in the reflection of his own eyes. He watched as another tear escaped, slid past his eyelashes, down his cheek, dripping onto his wrinkled shirt collar. He set the razor down on the counter and turned back to his room to put his socks and shoes on, although he wasn't sure where he would go.

Just as he slipped a foot into his shoe, the doorbell rang. Greg stood, forgetting that he only had one shoe on, and limped to the door.

"Who is it?" He called out, his voice weak.

"It's Beth and Anna," Beth's voice called back, and Greg opened the door.

"Huh... hi," Greg stammered, embarrassed seeing the twins' expressions when they saw him.

"Oh, Greg," Beth said. "Are you okay?"

Greg forced a half smile and nodded, pushing back the tears that he couldn't seem to control since the incident.

"We brought you some things," Anna said. "Can we come in and fix you some tea?"

"Um, the place," Greg motioned behind him. "It's kind of a mess."

"We're not worried about that at all," Beth said. "We actually need to talk to you about something."

Greg stood a little taller. He felt relieved that it wasn't just a pity call to check on him. Maybe it helped to feel needed. He stepped aside and held his arm out to invite the twins inside.

"Thank you," Beth said, squeezing his arm gently as she passed him. Anna carried two boxes wrapped with red and green ribbons. Greg realized that he might be a little bit hungry and tried to remember the last time he had a full meal. It was surely before the incident.

The twins headed to the kitchen and encouraged Greg to sit at the nearby table. Within minutes, they had prepared tea and platters of finger sandwiches, miniature quiches, small cakes, and fruit. They quickly cleared off the table, finding a new place for everything and set the delicious food in front of him before serving him a cup of peppermint tea.

"Peppermint tea to give you some pep," Beth winked at him as she poured it.

Greg thanked them and after they settled in with cups of tea of their own, he began to dig in, piling his small plate full of the tasty treats. Beth and Anna talked about the weather and about the town's holiday decorations along Main Street, as Greg sat and enjoyed the company and good food.

When he had finished his cup of tea, Beth poured him another.

Greg was starting to feel more alive. "I can't thank you enough. You have no idea how much I needed this," he said, happy that he could say all of that without breaking down into tears again.

"Oh, we figured you might," Beth winked.

"*Jah*, no one has seen you since that night, and we wanted to check on you," Anna said.

Greg looked down at his hands, now clasped in his lap. He blinked away the vision of blood that he instantly saw. He wondered if he would ever forget.

Anna continued and interrupted his thoughts. "So, we wanted to tell you that everything has been cleaned at the library now."

Beth nodded. "*Jah*, it looks good as new, Greg."

Greg continued to look down.

"Do you think you could come back?" Beth asked the question carefully.

Greg remained silent for what seemed like an eternity. He didn't know the answer to that question.

"You know, I think I would like to go to the theater tonight," he said instead.

Beth and Anna exchanged glances.

"I left my guitar there," Greg said.

"I see," Anna said, knowing that Francine's ex-husband, Damon, owned the theater. "Have you seen Damon since..." Her words trailed off because they all knew what she was referring to.

Greg lifted his face from his lap and shook his head, looking from one twin to another.

"I know you two have been friends for a long time," Beth said carefully.

"Yes, we have," Greg said. "When he and Francine separated, it was terrible. I was always in the middle. Damon thought I took Francine's side and she thought I took Damon's side. But, it wasn't true." Greg paused. "I didn't ever want to take a side."

"I can imagine that must've been tough for you," Anna said.

"Yes. It still is," Greg said, his voice cracking with emotion.

Anna and Beth exchanged glances again. Greg felt tired and wanted to go back to bed, but he suddenly remembered that the twins said they had something to talk to him about.

"So, what is it you wanted to talk to me about?" Greg asked, slumping in his chair.

Beth and Anna exchanged looks again. Beth cleared her throat before speaking.

"Well, Greg, we want to move forward with the holiday fundraising party. We feel like it's the right thing to do," she said.

Greg was floored. His mouth fell open.

"What? Are you serious? How could we celebrate in a place where Francine was murdered?"

"So, that's why we think we should…" Beth continued, looking over at Anna who nodded in agreement.

"It will help everyone put it behind them, and it's still a great cause," Anna said.

"This is preposterous! We don't even know who killed her. We were all there. And it happened…it happened while we were there!" Greg broke down crying. Anna stood to retrieve tissues for him from the box on the end table in the nearby living room.

"The sheriff has approved the party, Greg, if that makes any difference," Beth said. "He has collected all the evidence he needs."

Greg blew his nose into the tissue. His eyes red, he took a deep breath and asked a question that he almost feared the answer. "What evidence was there?"

Again, the sisters exchanged glances.

"Do you remember what they found that night, Greg?" Anna asked quietly.

"No," Greg said, leaning forward. "I don't."

There was an awkward moment of silence before Greg pleaded in a quiet voice, "Please tell me."

Beth reached out and held Anna's hand under the table.

"There was evidence in the restroom, Greg," Beth said.

Greg studied Beth's face. How could he not remember this?

"Go on," he said. "What evidence?"

"There were prints on the window and window frame where the killer escaped out of the bathroom window," Anna explained. "And the murder weapon was found under the bathroom sink."

Greg repeated the last part of the sentence as a question, "The murder weapon was found under the bathroom sink?"

Beth and Anna nodded.

"What was it?" Greg asked timidly.

There was a long pause before Beth leaned forward and answered, "It was an icicle."

Greg wondered if he was even awake. A slow chuckle escaped his lips and then before he knew it, he was fully overcome with laughter. Beth and Anna sat across the table from him, concerned looks on their faces.

When he finally was able to compose himself enough to speak, he said, "Isn't that ironic. Francine was killed in the mystery book section. Stabbed with an icepick that was left behind. How much more mysterious can you get?"

Beth and Anna nodded, polite smiles on their faces.

"That's not all, though, Greg," Anna said.

Greg ran his hands through his hair, still shaking off the last of the giggles.

"Okay, lay it on me. I can't imagine what else you're going to tell me."

"There was an open book on the floor near Francine's hand," Anna continued.

Beth interjected, "There was another note in it, Greg."

Greg leaned forward as if he were about to hear the biggest secret of his life. "What did it say?" he asked, his breath quickening.

"It said, *We have been more than patient. We are done playing games.*"

Chapter Nine

Beth and Anna agreed to drive to the theater and collect Greg's guitar for him. He wasn't quite ready to face the world just yet, and for some reason, he was really fixated on bringing his instrument back home. It didn't make sense to Beth, but she figured it was probably just part of the shock that he was experiencing.

"He was in pretty bad shape, huh?" Beth asked her sister.

"*Jah*, he was," Anna said. "I don't think we're going to be able to have that party unless this case is solved."

"I agree," Beth said. "And the clock is ticking. If it's not solved soon, there will be no hope for the library."

The buggy pulled up in front of the small theater, and the women stepped out, being careful not to slip on any icy patches. They approached the theater and pulled the handles on the front door. It was locked. They knocked on the door, but there was no answer.

"I guess no one is here," Anna said, turning to walk away.

"I thought I heard something just now," Beth said, cupping her hands and pressing against the dark painted glass in an attempt to see inside.

The door's lock turned and the door cracked open. Damon Waters stood on the other side.

"Can I help you?" he asked. "The theater is closed."

"Oh," Beth said, "We are actually here just to pick something up for a friend."

Damon didn't respond. Instead he waited for Beth to continue. Anna was quickly standing by her sister's side.

"It's Greg Wilson's guitar," Beth explained. "He said he left it here..."

Damon hesitated and then opened the door further, motioning for the sisters to come inside quickly. After they were both inside, he shut and fastened the door behind them.

"How is Greg doing?" Damon asked. "He hasn't answered his phone."

Beth thought that was odd. Greg mentioned that he hadn't heard from Damon since Francine had been murdered, but he was in a real state of shock so she didn't know who to believe.

Anna responded. "He's still recovering, for the most part," she said.

Beth and Anna had never been inside the theater, and Beth was fascinated with all of it. It smelled of strange incense and was dimly lit. The building was old and the audience seats were worn, but Beth thought that the small stage had a sort of personality and probably had a wonderful long history of shows.

"It's in my office," Damon said. He led the sisters to the right, behind a small concession counter. "I put it in here so it wouldn't go missing or get damaged."

As they walked into Damon's office, Beth noticed the walls were covered with movie theater posters, pictures of Cassidy, and drawings. Beth spotted right away a drawing of a single rose in a pot and was reminded of the vase with the sunflowers.

"Oh, did Cassidy draw this?" Beth asked, admiration in her voice.

"Yes, she did," Damon responded proudly. "She drew all of these. She's very talented."

"How is she doing, by the way?" Anna asked as Beth looked closely at the drawings.

"She'll be okay," Damon said. Beth noticed his demeanor change when Anna asked about Cassidy, and she couldn't quite put an explanation to it.

"Here's Greg's guitar," Damon said, reaching underneath the desk to grab it.

Out of the blue, Anna said, "I'm sorry for your loss, Mr. Waters."

Beth thought Damon looked confused and maybe a little panicked. He regained his composure and responded, "Well, Francine was Cass's mother, but that's all she was to me. She and I were not in a good place." He paused before continuing. "You know, her and Cass didn't even have that great of a relationship either. She was such a selfish woman. Everything was always about her."

He handed over the guitar.

"That's a shame," Anna said. "Well, thank you for this. I guess we'll get out of your hair now."

"Tell Greg that I said hello," Damon said. "I don't know why he couldn't come get this himself, but I hope he's okay."

"I think it was all pretty traumatic for him," Anna said. "He'll be okay with time, I'm sure."

Anna turned to Beth. "Are you ready to go, Beth?"

Beth heard Anna say the words, but she couldn't peel her eyes away from Cassidy's drawings. Her eyes quickly scanned each drawing, and they all had something in common. In the bottom right hand corner was Cassidy's signature.

Her name was signed in a mix of cursive and print. There was a long slender loop below the letter "y," and the letter "s" was always a printed curved line instead of a boxy cursive letter.

"Hey, Dad," Cassidy stood at the doorway. She looked at Anna and Beth and then looked back at Damon. "What's going on?" she asked, her eyebrows raised.

"Ah, nothing," Damon said. "These ladies came to get Greg's guitar."

"We were just leaving," Anna said, gently guiding Beth by the elbow.

As Beth passed Cassidy, she stopped. "I'm really impressed with your art," she told her.

Cassidy squinted her eyes and remained silent.

"Everything is really detailed and beautiful. Even your signature. Your handwriting is very unique," Beth continued.

Cassidy didn't blink an eye. "Thank you," she said. "My dream is to go to the New York Institute of Art and Design when I graduate from college."

"That's wonderful," Beth said.

"Okay, thanks again," Anna said, tugging on Beth's arm again. Beth turned around and faced Damon.

"One more thing, Mr. Waters," Beth said. "Did Greg mention the threatening letters he has been getting at the library?"

She felt Cassidy fidget next to her.

"No," Damon said. "I don't think he did. Why do you ask?"

"I don't know. When I looked at the letters, their handwriting was so unique." Beth paused and looked at Cassidy. "It looked a lot like your handwriting, actually. Isn't that weird?"

Anna gasped. "Beth!" she whispered loudly under her breath, grabbing Beth's arm less carefully this time and pulling her toward the door.

"My daughter had nothing to do with Francine's death," Damon yelled as they made a quick exit. "She has a full future ahead of her, I'll have you know. I won't let anything stand in the way of that. Especially not two nosy Amish women."

Anna yanked Beth one last time, and before she knew it, they were outside of the theater, piling into the buggy and heading for the sheriff's office.

Chapter Ten

B eth set the Brussel Sprouts Au Gratin on the table near Noah's seat. It was his favorite holiday vegetable dish, and she was surprising him with it a couple weeks early this year.

Abigail and Jeremiah and their daughter, Emma, and son, Jo, were playing cards on the floor in the living room before dinner was ready. Jonah walked in the door and greeted everyone with his typical big smile.

"*Wilkumme*, son!" Beth called out. "Come in, come in, and shut the door! Hang up your coat and come give your *Maem* a hug!"

Jonah hurried to his mom's side and wrapped his arms around her. "How are you? Are you feeling ready for the holiday?" he asked.

"Well, I have to say, it feels like there's so much chaos around this year's Christmas," Beth said.

"What would Christmas be without a little bit of chaos? I'm not sure it would feel right," Jonah said, with a wink.

"Well, I guess that's one way of looking at it," Beth laughed. "Dinner is almost ready. *Denki* for coming."

"I wouldn't miss it," Jonah winked and then joined Abigail, Jeremiah and the kids on the floor, butting his way into their game.

Noah came in through the back door, stomping his boots to shake off the snow onto the mat. "It smells *wunderbaar*," he exclaimed.

"Hi, *Dat*!" Abigail, Jeremiah and Jonah called out.

Beth kissed her husband on the cheek. "Go get cleaned up for supper. It's ready," she said.

As Noah stepped away, Abigail jumped up to help her mother with the final touches. As Abigail buttered rolls, Beth set the remaining dishes on the table.

"So, you never told me what you found out," Abigail said. "Who was arrested for Francine's murder?"

Beth wiped her hands on her apron. "Oh, you won't believe it," she said. "It's actually quite sad." Beth took a deep breath and glanced over to make sure the younger children were not in earshot.

"As it turns out, Francine was the one who was sending the letters. She was making her daughter, Cassidy, write the letters," she began.

"But, why would she want the library to close if she was working there?" Abigail asked.

"The whole thing was about Greg. She thought he was spineless. She told Cassidy that Greg ruined her life with her terrible job, but she really hated that he was still friends with her husband. So she wanted revenge. She wanted to ruin his life." Beth paused and leaned up against the counter. "And you know, she almost did."

Abigail gasped, "Wait, are you saying that Greg killed Francine?" Her eyes were wide and she shook her head. "I don't believe that for a minute," she said.

"Oh, no," Beth said. "Greg couldn't kill a fly," she chuckled.

"So, it was the daughter? How could that be?" Abigail said.

"No, it wasn't Cassidy either. The sheriff arrested Mr. Waters for first degree murder. He confessed when they put the cuffs on him," Beth said.

"Really?" Abigail gasped.

"Yes, why? Does that surprise you?" Beth asked, nonchalantly.

"Well, yes, of course it does," Abigail said. "For one, I'm still confused as to how it happened while we were there."

"Ah, yes, I know what you mean. That is the scariest part, honestly," Beth said. "The sheriff suspects that he sneaked in the same way that he went out."

"Through the window in the bathroom?" Abigail asked.

"Yes," Beth said. "Mr. Waters had some letters and voicemail recordings where his ex-wife was threatening to do whatever she could to destroy him and take away the one thing he loved the most."

"His daughter?" Abigail asked.

"No," Beth shook her head. "The theater."

Abigail wrinkled her brow.

"I guess he had lost his position serving as treasurer on the town council because Francine had sabotaged him by spreading terrible rumors," Beth continued.

Abigail was quiet.

"What are you thinking, *dochder*?" Beth asked.

"Something doesn't feel right," Abigail said.

"What do you mean?"

"Well, I'm confused how Mr Waters could have been nimble enough to get in and out of that bathroom window. It's not very big." Abigail said. "Weird that no one thought of that."

Abigail paused before continuing, "And then, what about the letter that they found lying next to her? Didn't she always mail the letters? It seems odd that she would be leaving a letter in a book this time."

Beth set down the mashed potatoes and looked at Abigail. Her mind was starting to make the connections and see what Abigail was seeing.

Suddenly, Beth gasped. "*Ach du lieva*, Mr. Waters didn't kill his ex-wife. It was Cassidy."

Abigail sighed. "I think the motive is still revenge, but I think it was a different kind of revenge. It was a daughter's revenge against a mother who was trying to ruin the lives of everyone around her."

Beth nodded. "He confessed, Abigail," she said softly. "Mr. Waters confessed to the murder."

"Well, you can talk to the sheriff tomorrow, but I don't know if anything would change," Abigail said.

Beth agreed.

Noah walked into the room, clean as a whistle. "Can I help with anything?" he asked.

"No, *denki*. I think we have everything on the table now," Beth answered. The family settled down at the table and said quiet prayers before filling their plates with delicious food. Beth's thoughts wandered to the drawings on the walls in Mr. Waters's office. She wondered how things would turn out for their family, and then she took a moment to look around the table at all the faces she loved. She wondered if she could ever take the blame for something so serious.

She shook her head. The thought was a waste of time. She knew she would never have to face something like that.

Follow Abigail in her journey in a new series, The Abigail Baker Mystery Series, as she moves to a new town and finds that solving crimes must run in her blood. You can find *The Abigail Baker Mystery Series* and more at marybbarbee.com

---

Just getting started in *The Amish Lantern Mystery Series* and want more? Visit marybbarbee.com and grab *Thick as Thieves* to find out how Anna and Beth solved their first murder case.

You can also get instant access to Anna and Beth's favorite recipes! Visit marybbarbee.com to grab your free copy of *The Amish Lantern Mystery Series Cookbook*.

A Note from the Author

---◈---

Thank you for reading *Christmas Chaos in Little Valley*! I must have written and rewritten so many parts of this story five times or more before I finally succumbed to calling it a complete work. When I began writing, this story was intended to be a full-length novel, but it seemed to have a mind of its own and fought against that through the entire creation process.

One of the things that didn't make it in the final manuscript were further exploring Francine and Damon's relationship struggles. Looking back, I think it's very likely that I wanted this story to have as little sadness as a murder mystery could have, considering the season.

Another piece of the manuscript that didn't make the final cut was further development of Jessica and Matthew's relationship, leading from A Blessing in Disguise. At first, I thought that would balance out the Francine and Damon relationship piece, then it felt more like a romance or women's fiction novel than a mystery. So, I decided to save that for the next book instead.

Overall, I think this story came together exactly as it was supposed to, and I thank you again for choosing *Christmas Chaos in Little Valley* to add to your book selection. If you enjoyed it, please consider leaving a review on Goodreads or Bookbub – or simply by recommending it to a friend!

With so much gratitude,

Mary B. Barbee

About the Author

Mary B. Barbee is the author of *The Amish Lantern Mystery Series* and *The Abigail Baker Mystery Series*. As an avid fan of all mystery and suspense in print, on television and in film, Mary B. believes the best mystery is one where the suspect changes throughout the story, keeping the audience guessing. She enjoys providing an exciting escape for a few hours with stories her readers can't put down - and always with a surprise ending.

When not writing, Mary B. is either playing a couple sets of tennis or a strategy board game with her two witty daughters and her kindly competitive mother. The four of them share a home in the Inland Northwest in the beautiful town of Spokane, Washington with their really cute - but sometimes naughty - chihuahua.

Mary loves to hear from her readers. Connect at:
mary@marybbarbee.com
www.facebook.com/marybbarbee
Instagram: @marybbarbee
www.marybbarbee.com

More Books to Read By Mary B. Barbee

THE AMISH LANTERN MYSTERY SERIES

Thick As Thieves – Book 1

Robberies are running rampant in Little Valley, and the quiet small-town lives of the Amish community are suddenly thrown into chaos.

Secrets in Little Valley – Book 2

With the bishop's daughter suddenly missing and a new sheriff in town, Anna and Beth find themselves roped into solving another mystery in their small town.

Saving Grace – Book 3

The Amish community in Little Valley is facing big changes, and big threats, with tourism booming. It becomes clear that some of the new businesses want control of the market, and it looks like they are willing to go to great lengths to get it.

Good Intentions – Book 4

Hazel Thompson is found dead in Little Valley's now-famous Amish Inn, and there's a long list of suspects with plenty of motive.

A Blessing in Disguise – Book 5

Jessica McLean opens shop to find a man has been left for dead on the floor of her diner. Could the crime could be related to Jessica's new relationship with their beloved Matthew Beiler?

Christmas Chaos in Little Valley - Book 6

Beth finds out that the Little Valley library is shutting its doors due to a lack of funding and very disturbing anonymous threats.

———◦———

THE ABIGAIL BAKER MYSTERY SERIES
Blind Faith – Prequel

Abigail's excitement for her new home is replaced by doom and gloom when she finds out that an unexplained murder has rocked the residents of her new town. And not unusual to her, it's the Amish community that is suspect number one.

**Grab your free e-copy of Blind Faith at:
marybbarbee.com/blindfaith**

Where Fear Ends – Book 1

A town councilman is found dead by the side of the road in the Amish community of Abigail Baker's new hometown.

A Multitude of Sins – Book 2

When secret notes containing serious threats are unveiled, Abigail wonders if the latest victim could have been hiding a multitude of sins.

A Wing and a Prayer – Book 3 ~ COMING SOON!

THE PUPCAKE MYSTERY SERIES
Cupcakes and Corruption – Prequel

Battling empty-nest syndrome, Eliza finds solace in the company of her adorable chihuahua, Pupcake, and her dreams of opening a quaint coffee shop. Little does she know that her talent for baking and nurturing also extends to amateur sleuthing.

Grab your free e-copy of Cupcakes and Corruption at: marybbarbee.com/pupcakeprequel

Sweet Suspicion – Book 1

The charming town of Copeland is buzzing with excitement as Eliza and her adorable chihuahua, Pupcake, open their new coffee shop. But when a body is discovered on the premises, the duo must put down their baking tools and pick up their detective hats.

Confections and Clues – Book 2 – Coming Valentine's Day 2025

Eliza and Pupcake's lakeside getaway takes a dark turn when they stumble upon a body. With a secretive small town and a case no one wants solved, Eliza's sweet retreat quickly turns into another mystery. Can she and Pupcake crack the case before the killer's trail goes cold?

Recipe for Reckoning – Book 3 ~ COMING SOON!

Find excerpts, purchase links and more at
www.marybbarbee.com

www.ingramcontent.com/pod-product-compliance
Lightning Source LLC
Chambersburg PA
CBHW022042170626
46808CB00003B/1322